I0780494

GRAVESIDE PRESS

ELIZABETH GUILT

I met Heather during a wet lunch-break. My best mate
and I were holed up under the staircase, playing a tape over
and over to figure out the lyrics of the opening track. The
original record sleeve probably had the words written out,
but Steve's brother wouldn't let him touch it.

"Something and eyeballs?" suggested Steve.

"Hmm. Does sound like eyeballs."

The words were impenetrable, apart from the bit about
wanting to know. When it hit the chorus, I just sang any
old nonsense.

"I am you, Shan! And I'll lose yer. I am you! Shan!"

Steve dug me hard in the ribs.

"What?"

He nodded. A girl I didn't recognise was crouched

down, peering at us under the stairs.

"Hey! What're you listening to?"

"A band from Boston. No one you'll know." Steve had a theory that girls—especially girls with perms—had terrible taste in music.

I held out my half of the headphones and she scooted over.

We'd reached a particularly spiky bit of guitar, and I saw Steve crank the volume up. Her eyes widened, but she didn't scream or back away. Steve looked grudgingly impressed and let the music run to the next track.

Left out, I sat in silence, watching the girl's tight curls bob as she nodded along. Her eyebrows rose, and I wondered if that was where the whispery vocals went into a sudden scream.

"That's amazing! Would you copy it for me? I'll bring a blank in tomorrow."

She was speaking to both of us, but I jumped in. "Sure! I'll run you one off tonight." Steve had already agreed to lend me the tape to copy for myself.

"Thank you! I'll bring a blank to swap."

I was usually tongue-tied if any of the girls in my class spoke to me, never mind someone whose name I didn't even know. If I'd stopped to think, I'd have got nervous and probably said something stupid.

"Nah, bring me a copy of something you like instead."

She smiled. She had the most beautiful smile I'd ever seen.

"I'm Heather."

I wrote the track listing out carefully, copying from Steve's brother's messy scrawl. It was a short album, and I spent a long time wondering what to put on the B-side for Heather. Eventually, I chose The Cure album I'd got for Christmas. It was already a few years old, but it was one of the few legit recordings I owned. When I taped Steve's album for myself, I put The Cure on the second side of that, too, to have the same experience as Heather when I listened to it. Sliding my tapes half an inch along the shelf made space for the new one at the right point in the alphabet.

I had no idea how to find Heather. I didn't know which class she was in or where she hung out so walked round school with the tape in my pocket, ready, in case I passed her in a corridor. At lunch, despite sunshine and the promise of football, I sat under the staircase and tried not to look like I was waiting.

"Hey, Stuart!"

Her voice made me jump. I held out the tape, suddenly

too shy to say anything.

"Oh wow, you have such neat writing!" She slung her bag off her shoulder. As she rummaged, it clattered like it was full of loose cassettes. The one she handed me had no case and had 'MIXTAPE FOR STUART' scribbled over the torn label.

"I didn't know what you'd have already," she said, "so I made a mix of songs I really like. I'm sorry there's no track list. I don't know what half of them are."

I was fifteen. Unlabelled tapes, tapes out of cases, cases out of order... All these things filled me with horror. Part of me was appalled and disappointed. The other part looked at Heather and melted, because this pretty girl had spent her evening making me a mixtape she hoped I'd like. I was confused, and excited, and desperate to listen to it.

The bell rang. Heather waved uncertainly and went up the stairs.

I shot out of class and jammed the tape into my personal stereo. A melancholy guitar sang, and I turned my face to the sky, letting the thin drizzle blur my eyes as droning vocals kicked in. When the song ended, I was almost dizzy, heart racing, wondering if Heather was walking home listening to the tape I'd made for her. The next track on her mix started with a bump a little way in; it was disorientating, with sections that sounded like they were played backwards, the singer's voice powerful and strident. It ended abruptly and dropped into a riff I knew well.

At home, I brushed off my mum's attempts at conversation, went straight up to my room, and laid on my bed until the ninety-minute mixtape ended. I recognised a few songs, but most were new to me. Some were brilliant: off the wall raging voices, screaming guitars, surprisingly tender melodies. The tape was a rollercoaster, and I loved it. When Mum shouted me down for dinner, I ate as quickly as I could and went back to listen to it again.

I wanted to know about the songs. I wanted to talk to Heather about them. I wanted to listen to them *with* her.

I went to school early, hoping to spot Heather's bright curls somewhere. I even approached a group of girls I thought were in her class, to ask if they knew where I could find her, then bottled it when their carefully indifferent gazes swept me from hair to shoes. When we changed lessons mid-morning, I looked constantly among the sea of grey jumpers and white shirts, hoping to see her. After lunch, I was unwinding my headphones under the stairs when Steve snapped his fingers in front of me.

"What?"

"Get a grip, Stu. Come and kick a ball about."

"What?"

"You're waiting for that girl, aren't you?"

"Heather."

"Yeah. If she likes you, she'll find you. You won't impress her hanging around."

"But…"

"Trust me."

He shoved me towards the door.

I did trust Steve. He didn't panic when girls spoke to him. He'd even been on a date over Christmas. I wasn't sure he was right, but I figured he was doing his best and spent the rest of the break playing football.

He was right: Heather found me. She was waiting outside the gate after school.

"Hey, Stuart."

"Hi!"

I ripped my headphones off, then stood awkwardly, thinking I should tell her I liked the mixtape. I should say something interesting about it. I should pick out a really cool track or talk about one of the ones I already knew…

Heather looked at me expectantly.

"I loved your mix! It made me want to listen to it with you, so we could talk about the songs." As soon as the words were out, I wanted to bite them back. I hadn't meant it to come out sounding so weird. And she'd probably think I was being pushy, and...

"That's cool. I love listening to music with someone else."

"You do?" Steve and I often listened to music together, but I hadn't thought it was a girl thing. Heather didn't seem like other girls, though.

"Yeah. You could come back to mine, if you want?"

"That'd be great."

Heather hitched her bag onto her shoulder and set off towards the big estate. I hurried after her.

After an awkward silence, I started talking about The Cure. She'd put a Cure song on her mixtape, so she must like them, and they were my favourite band. I'd read an interview with Robert Smith where he talked about loving Hubba Bubba bubble-gum, and how he always bought the Beano, and how he had a really cool electronic calculator that was also an address book... I trailed to a halt, realising I was just babbling.

Heather turned. "Do you read about bands a lot? Where did you read that?"

I'd backed myself into a corner. I didn't want to lie, but I also didn't want to admit that I asked for the *Smash Hits Yearbook* every Christmas. *Smash Hits* was for kids, even if they had interviewed Robert Smith. If only I'd read it in something credible, like *NME*. "Not that much," I mumbled.

"I never read music magazines." She didn't seem to notice my hesitation. "I don't care about the bands; I just want to listen to the music."

"But how do you know when new stuff's coming out?"

She shrugged. "I don't. I find things sooner or later. Or someone tells me."

There was a little fizz in my chest: I knew something. "There's a new Cure album coming out next month."

Heather's brilliant smile lit up the dull afternoon. "See? Do you know anyone who'll buy it?"

"I will."

"You?" She looked stunned, almost scornful. "You buy albums?"

"Not usually." I wanted to, but I couldn't afford it. "I've been saving up."

"The Cure are really your thing, then?"

They were my favourite band. Saying so out loud suddenly seemed childish, like telling her my favourite animal was a tiger. "I guess so. But I like loads of other stuff, too. I don't know many people who buy albums—most of mine are copies from Steve."

"Steve? Oh, the other guy under the stairs?"

"Yeah. His brother's got a job. He buys loads of stuff." She winked. "Useful guy to know."

Heather walked towards an ugly concrete house. There was an old mattress and some sacks of rubble where the front garden should be. She let herself in, headed straight upstairs without shouting *hello* to anyone, and opened a door that spelled out 'Heather' in tumbling pink bears. Her room was tiny, just a bed along one wall, a bedside table, and a chest of drawers. The floor was ankle-deep in cassettes.

"Sit down." She dumped her bag on top of the tapes—right on top of them—and waved at the bed. I was in a girl's bedroom, which already felt weird, and now I was perched primly on her bed, rucksack on my knees, trying to burrow my school shoes under the drifts of tapes.

"What do you want to listen to? What did you like on my mix?"

My mind went blank. I had her mixtape with me, of course I did. I hadn't listened to anything else since she handed it over. I wanted to hear what she thought of each track.

Instead, I said, "That opening song. The rainy one. Who was that?"

Her face lit up. "Rainy?"

"Well, I thought it sounded rainy. Maybe it was just

raining when I first heard it.”

“No, I see what you mean. My cousin bought it a couple of weeks ago. He lives in Manchester, says they’re the next big thing. I really want to hear more of their stuff.”

“Me too,” I said, and I meant it.

Her smile made me dizzy. “Yeah, that’s why I put it first. It sounds like a beginning. Maybe it’s our beginning.”

I nodded, entranced. I didn’t know what we were beginning. I didn’t know anything.

“Not sure. Too much bass?”

“Yeah.” Heather ripped the tape from the player and grabbed another. She fast-forwarded a bit, then held the play button halfway-down, so the music squealed past at double speed until she found what she wanted. “How about this?”

I never knew where to look when Heather played me something. She always watched my reaction, willing me to like it, or to feel the same way about it she did. Meeting her eyes left me too exposed, and was too scary, so I usually stared at the little wheels going round inside the boombox.

“It sounds old. Cool, but old. Maybe one of those New York bands from the seventies?”

It had taken me weeks to feel brave enough to say

what I thought. I was terrified of saying the wrong thing—of liking something dreadful—and daunted by Heather's amazing memory. She knew hardly any bands, but she knew every song on every tape. And she could find anything, even half-songs, taped from the radio onto cracked cassettes and left under piles of laundry. She claimed she'd never heard The Smiths until I sang the opening of *The Queen Is Dead*.

"Oh, yeah. I got that from the footwell of my cousin's car. Boxing Day last year. I like it." She found her copy, and we listened to a few songs.

Steve never believed Heather and I just sat and played tapes.

"So, what happened?" he demanded the day after I first went to Heather's house.

Nothing, I told him. I'd sat on Heather's bed and listened to music, much like he and I did.

"Did you kiss her?" he asked, and I said no, of course not. He rolled his eyes, like not kissing her was the weirdest thing in the world.

He asked again and again, as I went to Heather's more often.

"You must have kissed her by now. Why haven't you kissed her?" If I went round his house after school, he just went on about it. I spent more time at Heather's. Even at the end of April when it was cold, and her parents had turned off the heating, we huddled under her duvet and pushed tape after tape into the player.

"Kissed her yet?" hissed Steve every morning. I told him each day that it wasn't like that.

Until, suddenly, it was like that.

"Come into town with me? After school, I mean. We can get the bus."

"Why?"

"I want to buy the new Cure album."

Heather nodded. "Sure."

I'd spent nothing in the previous few weeks and had done chores in exchange for extra pocket money. Even then, I'd borrowed a couple of pounds from my mum, just to be sure.

In the record shop, I went straight to C on the racks. I wondered whether to tell Heather then and there; instead, I picked up the second album quietly while she wasn't looking. She seemed lost, dazzled, among the racks of tapes, records, and even CDs. Her fingers trailed absently along the shelves, touching each album gently. She didn't flick through artists she knew or check prices. Her nail snagged on the beaded line of a tape's plastic wrapping.

"So much music," she whispered. "All sealed up. Dead. Can't you feel it? This place is a mortuary for songs."

After I'd paid, we ran for the bus. We could have shared headphones and listened the way we had done under the stairs. But this was an occasion. I wanted to sit in Heather's room and listen, *properly* listen, to it.

We never went to my house. Heather never asked, and I never offered. My mother would've expected us to sit in the living room and talk to her about school. She would have been horrified at the idea of us going upstairs unsupervised.

It was always Heather who chose the tapes, Heather who pressed play or pause or stop. She pulled out the new cassette, dropping the box and its splodgy blue-green sleeve notes to the floor without looking, and I decided, for once, to leave them. I put my arm round her and smiled into her hair as the first dramatic chords spilled from the speakers.

We laid perfectly still and listened. For once Heather didn't bounce up, saying, "Oh, wait, what about this?" or, "Hey, that reminds me!" She just let it play. Was she caught up in it, too? Or did she do it for me? I didn't know. But it felt perfect, and the music washed over me. The whispery vocals made me suddenly aware of how much I loved Heather; how much I would always love her.

Whatever happened.

Abruptly, during a skittery, almost nursery-rhyme song, she turned and kissed me. I'd never been kissed before, and the sudden force of it was overwhelming. Whenever Steve had asked about kissing Heather, the whole idea had made me feel weird and squirmy. But now, with her lips on mine, nothing seemed complicated. My arms curled around her, her fingers tight in the hair at the back of my neck. The sensation of her body stretched against mine, blended seamlessly with the music as we kissed, and listened, and kissed again.

When the button clicked up at the end of side A, I jumped. All the awkwardness suddenly landed back on me. What should I say or do now? Would she notice that I'd got...

Heather sprawled over the edge of the bed, flipping the tape. She left one arm across my chest and pulled herself back up to lie on top of me, pressed against me in a way that said she knew, of course she knew, and it was all right.

We listened to side B, lying together, her breath close on my face. When the button snapped up again, neither of us moved. I didn't want to.

Eventually, Heather murmured against my neck, "This album will always be you."

"What?" I'd heard her, but I wanted her to explain. I

wanted her to say it again.

She didn't. A moment later, she pushed herself up onto her elbows and said, "That album isn't like their other stuff, is it?"

No. It wasn't. I wondered how I'd feel if I'd heard it by myself or had listened to it with Steve. Would I have been disappointed? I couldn't tell. This would always be the perfect album, the one I listened to with my arms around Heather.

She carried on, as if I'd answered. "I like that. No one wants another album that's just more of the same. I like it when a band does something new."

"I think I like it. I want to listen to it again."

"Now?" she asked.

I looked at my watch. Crap. I was going to be late home. Mum was probably already wondering where I was.

"I should go. Mum will be getting worried." But I didn't move.

"Already? It's not late."

"You know." I shrugged, trying to sum up the trouble I'd be in if I wasn't home for dinner, the dreariness of my mum lecturing me about punctuality, and my dad shouting about ingratitude. Perhaps she didn't know.

I took the tape from the stereo, tucked it into its case, and put it in my pocket as I left.

Heather looked so sad. The following day, as soon as I saw her in school, I handed her the copy I'd made. I'd written out the track listing, even though I knew she didn't care. The case would end up on her floor, lost under her bed, discarded as soon as she got home. But I saw her eyes light up when I handed it over, and that was enough.

"You free after school?"

I shook my head. "Football match. Tomorrow?"

"See you tomorrow."

I still had the second tape, the one I hadn't told Heather about. It was the band—her band, I always thought—the one her cousin had found in Manchester. The rainy band from the mixtape she'd made me. I had bought their first album for her. I kind of wanted to hold on to it, keeping it for a special moment. Giving her it now felt too soon, too much—but I couldn't risk her hearing it somewhere else. I wanted to be the one to share it with her.

Next time I followed Heather home after school, I waited till we reached her room, and then told her to close her eyes.

"Why?" She looked suddenly wary and (unnervingly) frightened.

"Nothing bad! I just brought you a present. A surprise."

"A present?" Her face turned hard and suspicious. "What present? Why?"

I opened my mouth to snap back that I wished I hadn't bothered, and realised her eyes were filling with tears. Her expression was unreadable, but was a million miles from the excitement I'd hoped for, and the disappointment stung. Miserably, I slipped the tape from my pocket and crouched to push it into her boombox. I stayed there, hunched, as the leader-tape hissed through.

The hiss grew louder, becoming a long, slow drum fade-in that once again reminded me of rain. Faint guitar noise chittered until a baseline began to pulse, and then a shimmering shower of high notes rippled out through the speakers.

Heather sucked in a breath. "This is them, isn't?"

I nodded, still with my back to her and no idea if she was looking at me.

"Their album?"

I nodded again. "I wanted to share it with you. I wanted to make you sm... sm..." My words stuck; my throat squeezed closed.

"Oh."

It was a tiny, soft sound, but it was very close to my face. Heather was leaning over, leaning off her bed, and reaching down to kiss me. Pushing my school jacket off my shoulders, pulling me up on top of her. Unbuttoning my shirt, reaching her hands inside my collar, along my shoulders, to lace her fingers round the back of my neck. She kissed me again, and again, her lips moving along with the words she'd picked up already.

I wanted to give her everything she wanted.

One of us must have turned the tape over. By the end of side B, we were lying still, tangled together, under the duvet. The final song ended with a guitar solo that went on and on. I wanted it to last forever if it meant I could lie suspended in this moment. When the last notes faded away, neither of us spoke. The house was silent, even the road outside and the neighbour's crying baby were quiet. Perhaps the world had stopped. Perhaps there was nothing left but the circle of my arms around Heather and the warmth of our bodies pressed against each other. When I kissed her gently on the cheek, she smiled, and the world began to turn again.

Heather leaned to turn the tape over. I rolled with her, arms around her, and the susurration of the opening track filled the room.

She curled against me. "This song... At the start, it's like someone breathing out. Relaxing. Like letting all your worries go or leaning back in the bath."

I squeezed her shoulders. Basking in the glow of her

skin, my worries seemed impossibly remote. Nothing mattered but Heather and the music.

We laid whispering about the songs, listening intently.

"That's such a weird noise. The guitars sound almost, I dunno. Squelchy?"

"I think it's playing backwards."

"What?" She jerked up onto her elbow. "What do you mean?"

"I mean, if you record stuff on tape, and then play the tape backwards, it sounds kind of like this."

Her eyes were wide open. "How do you play a tape backwards? Play and rewind at the same time?" I caught her wrist as she reached down.

"Nah, that'll more likely snap it. Copy the song onto an old tape you don't care about, and I'll show you. It kind of destroys the tape."

Heather swiped up a huge, baggy sweatshirt from the floor, pulled it on, and flopped down beside the boombox.

Under the covers, I watched as she switched the tapes around. The frayed cuffs hung down past her fingers, and her curls hid her face.

She copied the song and looked up expectantly.

"We'll need scissors, and Sellotape."

Her face fell. "I don't know if we've got any. I'll check."

Looking up at her ceiling, I played the past hour over in

my mind. At school, people talked about what they'd done with girls, boasting about how far they'd got, but I already knew I wouldn't mention this. Not even to Steve, who would come back with a million questions. I'd never be able to explain the feeling of lying in bed, my arms around Heather, quietly happy. Perhaps it was because I loved her.

"This is all I could find."

She'd come back in quietly, and she made me jump. She had a big pair of kitchen scissors, a roll of what looked like insulation tape, and some glue.

"Oh my God, did your parents see you with just a sweatshirt on? Won't you get in trouble?"

She shrugged. "They're out. Will this do?"

The roll of tape looked old, fluff sticking to its edges.

"The glue might be better. Let's try it."

I grabbed the tape and went over to the chest of drawers.

"Okay. So, pull the tape out, like this."

Heather sat on the bed, watching, and realisation hit me. Cheeks bright red, I struggled back into my school shirt and trousers, feet sliding on tapes, silently willing her to look the other way. She laughed at me, but in a nice way.

I snipped the magnetic tape, flipped it over, and used a tiny dab of glue to hold the ends together.

"Once this dries, I'll wind it along, keeping the twist in it. Then when we play it, it'll sound backwards."

"Why?"

"It just does."

"How do you know?"

"It's something Steve and I messed around with. Playing things backwards. Playing speech backwards. Trying to say stuff so that when you play it backwards it sounds normal again."

"Wow, can you do that?

"Nah, not very well. We had a fun few days trying."

"The glue will be dry now."

It didn't really seem like we'd left it long enough, but what the hell; I started winding the wheels. Heather rummaged in her schoolbag for a couple of pencils and we did it between us, winding the wheels round while I kept the twist in the tape. When I guessed we'd gone far enough, I rewound it and played.

A few seconds after the music started, Heather started to laugh. I was just behind her.

"Isn't that...?"

"Yes!"

"It's the one before..."

The previous song, a bit halting and glitchy, but unmistakable.

"So, track four is basically just track three backwards!"

It seemed like the funniest thing we'd ever heard.

Heather wanted to try playing her voice backwards. She was quick and was soon flipping the tape. As it got dark outside, there was a strangled squeal from the boombox.

She laughed. "Ah, well. I guess it snapped. Are you hungry?"

I'd told my mum a half-story about visiting a friend and not to expect me back for dinner. She'd assumed it was Steve, and I hadn't corrected her.

"Really hungry, actually."

Heather pulled on a pair of jeans. "Let's go to the chippy."

We shared chips, eating from the paper as we walked back to hers. I guessed her parents still weren't home, but we still went straight up to her room.

"I should go soon."

She kissed me. "Do you want to come round on Saturday?"

On Saturday, I was supposed to be watching the football with my dad. I didn't care. "Yes. Yes, please."

As I got up to go, I found the cassette case in my pocket. I dropped it on the floor with everything else.

I didn't see Heather on Friday. Steve had changed his question from "Have you kissed her yet?" to "Why are you still bothering with her?" I told him I enjoyed hanging out with her and asked if he wanted to listen to my new album after school. He said no, he was busy, and I was almost relieved. When I went round to Heather's late on Saturday morning, there was no answer. Maybe she'd meant afternoon? I should've checked.

I caught the bus into town and wandered round. Standing in front of the jeweller's window, I saw a tiny musical note on a gold chain, and wondered if Heather would like it. Not that I could afford it—and she'd been so strange before about presents. I spent a while at the listening posts in the record shop, but nothing grabbed me. Walking back to her house, a car pulled up at the lights with music blaring: spiky and driving, yelp-y vocals, then a two-note guitar solo like an ambulance siren. I listened as it drove away.

There was still no answer at Heather's. Eventually, I headed home, making up a story about where I'd been.

It wasn't that I didn't want to tell Mum about her. Well, it kind of was. Talking about Heather felt too personal, too dangerous. Mum would want to meet her and make a big thing out of it. Just imagining her on the phone to Aunty Karen—*Ooh, and Stuart's got a girlfriend*—made me feel sick. I wanted to get used to the idea myself before I told anyone.

I tried to make up explanations for where Heather was, but I was disappointed and angry. I'd missed the game with my dad because I'd been hoping to spend the whole day with her, and instead just trudged around by myself.

Driving to Gran's on Sunday, we went along the main road beside the estate, and I automatically looked towards Heather's house. For once, there was a car in the drive—a van, really. I wondered if that meant her dad was at home. The van was still there on Monday after school when I walked past. Should I go and knock? Somehow, the idea of the father I'd never met answering the door was terrifying. Maybe he wouldn't know who I was. Worse, maybe he *would*. After standing, uncertain, for about ten minutes I turned miserably home.

After school the next day, I heard her voice behind me.

"Hey, Stuart! Listen to this!" She was holding out a pair of headphones.

"Where were you on Saturday?"

"What?" The smile dropped off her face.

"On Saturday. You weren't in. I waited all day."

"I was at my cousin's."

"You invited me round. I wasted the whole day."

She glared at me, eyes hard, but didn't explain. All I wanted was for her to say sorry, tell me it was a misunderstanding, explain why she'd let me down. She said nothing, and it was only as she turned away that I realised she was close to crying.

"Heather!" I grabbed her shoulders, but she shook me off. "Heather, I'm sorry!"

Why was I apologising? I needed her to say something—anything—to show me she cared.

"My dad said we were going to see my cousins." Her voice sounded small and sad.

"Couldn't you tell him you were busy?

She whirled round. "Couldn't I? You can't even tell your mam you're going to be late for tea."

There was a weird hooting noise. Behind me, Steve and a couple of others were laughing, clearly enjoying watching Heather and me having a fight.

"Just kiss her," someone yelled across the road.

Staring at the ground I muttered, "I'm sorry about them."

"They're not your fault. Come home with me? Please?"

I wanted to follow her. I wanted to walk away. I wanted to shake her until she understood how much she'd upset me. I wanted to kiss her. I wanted Steve to stop making everything worse.

I nodded. "Okay."

Heather rushed up the stairs and into a room that was even more chaotic than usual. There were clothes everywhere, drawers hanging open. Shuffling across the room, I realised that a lot of the cassettes were cracked and broken open. An odd, chilly feeling dripped down my back. Heather was careless of her tapes in all the ways I cared about, but not like that.

She sat a little apart from me on the bed, leaning down to push play on whatever was already in the boombox. An old, old album; she just let it run, closing her eyes.

When the album ended, I touched her shoulder, very gently, and she jumped, eyes snapping open. I whisked my hand away.

"Are you all right?"

Her lips twitched, as if words wanted to escape, and I thought again that her eyes looked like she might cry.

"I'm fine. I... No. I'm fine."

For the first time, the silence between us felt awkward. Last time, she'd pulled my clothes right off me. Now I couldn't even work out how to give her a hug. I raised my arm a little to see if she wanted to come and lean against me, but she didn't move.

"I went into town on Saturday," I mumbled, desperate for anything to say. Heather stiffened, as if she thought I was starting another fight, so I rushed on. "I went into the record shop. I listened to a load of stuff." I reeled off a list of bands, trying to fill the space.

"Any good?" Her question was wooden, but at least she said something.

"No, not really. Nothing exciting. Oh, except there was this one song—not even in the record shop. I heard it playing from a car radio while I was walking back. Do you know this?"

I paused, trying to figure out how to make the sound that I could still hear in my head come out of my mouth. I didn't know the lyrics, there wasn't even much melody; just a spiky rhythm, a quality of sound, and that piercing two-note guitar. I sputtered out something that sounded nothing like it.

She shook her head. "No idea, sorry."

"Yeah, it didn't sound anything like that. I really liked it, though."

"You didn't get any of the words?"

"No."

"I hate it when that happens."

"Yeah, I usually end up singing bits and pieces at Steve's brother. He's really good at figuring out what I mean. I just haven't seen him recently."

"Sorry."

"What?"

"Because you've been coming here instead of hanging out with Steve." Her voice was flat and dead again.

"I'd rather hang out with you than Steve. He's been such a wanker recently. Always asking about whether we've..." I realised too late what I was saying.

She looked at me, hair falling across face. "And did you tell him?"

"No!"

"Why not?"

"What?" Her question startled me. Had she wanted me to brag to Steve? She stared at me like it was a test. "Because it was nothing to do with him, I didn't want to talk about you like you were just another.... Just another goal to score, or something. I couldn't bear to share even that much of you with him." The last bit surprised even me, and I felt my voice shaking.

Heather carried on staring at me, her eyes huge. It seemed like an invitation, and I leaned in, putting my hand on her cheek the way I'd seen people do in films. She closed her eyes, her head against my palm, and I pushed forward to kiss her. I knew something was wrong, I knew it, but I kept hoping that somehow, she'd understand how much she meant to me and kiss me back.

She went rigid, and when I pulled away, her eyes were wide. She looked terrified.

"Heather, what's wrong? What's the matter?" She felt like a rag doll in my hands, and she didn't reply.

"Heather?" Her stillness made me want to shake her, shake her out of it, make her tell me what was happening. But tears were spilling down her face, and I didn't know what to say. I felt useless, hating myself, and almost hating her for doing this.

When she spoke, she was so quiet I couldn't hear.

"What?"

"I'm sorry."

"What for? What's the matter?"

"I'm sorry."

She hunched her knees up, then slumped over, curling into the duvet and turning her back to me. She made no sound, but her shoulders were shaking. Caught in the moment, I stood beside her, wanting to help but completely at sea. She'd flinched away from me whenever I went near her, and she didn't want to talk.

"Do you want me to stay?" I asked, not even sure what I was hoping for. She didn't reply and, after a while, I picked my way across her room. There was a little space cleared on her bedside table, and in it was the album I'd given her, sitting in its box.

I scrubbed at my eyes as I let myself out of Heather's house.

At school, I spent my lunch break under the stairs. I'd never known how to find Heather; she'd always found me; all I could do was make myself easy to find. Folded up into the furthest corner, I put my headphones on and flicked the Vs at Steve when he came by to take the piss. He ignored me during the match, and I went home angry and knotted up. Mum ruffled my hair and asked about my day, then gave me a hug and stopped asking.

On Thursday lunchtime, I prowled around, peering into classrooms, trying to look for Heather without drawing attention. People sniggered as I walked away. There had never been so many people in my school, so many faces, and none of them the one I wanted. In the end, I slunk back under the stairs and turned the volume up to drown everything out.

All the songs sang to me of Heather.

She caught me on the way home. She wasn't in uniform.

"Heather! What are you doing here?"

"Waiting for you." She fidgeted with her headphones, black jewellery flashing on her wrists. No—glossy audio tape wrapped around both wrists. It glinted in the sun, and I wanted to tell her how pretty it looked.

"Were you in school?"

"No."

I waited for her to explain. She didn't. Instead, she pulled a couple of cassettes out of her pocket.

"I got these." She held them out, like an offering. They were still in their shrink-wrap, shiny new from the shop. "Do you want to come back with me? Just to listen to them?"

Of course I did. The memory of us laying together listening to The Cure burning in my mind, and I wanted to feel close and happy and loved, the way I had then.

"Where did you suddenly get the money for these from?"

She shrugged and walked faster.

"Are these more recommendations from your cousin?"

"No, I haven't seen him."

"Weren't you there on Saturday?" My voice came out much more accusing than I meant.

"What? Different cousins. No. I just liked the pictures on these."

"Heather," I began, and she half-turned to look at me. I couldn't form the words, couldn't work out how to ask again. Something was wrong, something was making Heather different, and I wanted to know what had happened. I wanted to see her smile again. I wanted...

"Oh, fuck." She stopped dead.

"What?"

"Stuart, I'm sorry. You have to go. My dad's back." The van was parked across the driveway, one wheel hanging off the kerb.

"Why? Doesn't he…"

"I'm sorry. Please. Go home."

"Okay. Fine." It wasn't fine. It wasn't fine at all and I wanted her to know that. But I wanted to keep her near me for a minute more.

"What was it you wanted to play me the other day? After school?"

"What? Oh. Never mind. I'll put it in a mix for you." She backed away for a few steps, then stood, watching me. I headed off without saying goodbye, then crept back to watch her head into her house. She didn't. Head down, headphones back on, she walked right past it and disappeared round the bend; I wondered about following her. When I went home, I stayed up too late finishing a tape for her, full of all the things I couldn't work out how to say myself.

She wasn't in school the next day, either, so I made up some nonsense reason to go to the school office and managed to sneak a look at the registers while the secretary was busy on the phone. Heather had been marked absent the past three days. The van was still there at home-time, but I thought about knocking on her door anyway, asking if she was okay. Instead, I went home and laid by myself, listening to the albums we'd enjoyed together, and longing to have her beside me.

On Saturday, Mum had jobs for me, even though I explained I had to go and see a friend. Her answer was, "Your friend will still be there this afternoon." I bolted ham sandwiches at lunch and ran across town. The van was gone, so I shot up the driveway and knocked on the door.

There was no answer.

I knocked. Knocked again. Waited.

Was that a flicker of movement, just visible through the pane of bubbly, cracked glass?

No one came, and eventually I turned to go. The van's tyres had gouged the patchy grass. Sticking up from the mud and gravel was a corner of black plastic and I picked at it, worrying that someone was watching me from the house. The cassette was shattered and mangled, as if it had been run over, its shiny black guts crushed and filthy. It was a cheap C90, the sort that piled up in drifts on Heather's floor. I stuffed it into my pocket.

Back home, I laid it on my desk wondering if I could wind the magnetic tape out and put it in a new cassette.

Even if it didn't work, it gave me something to do, something that meant I felt a little closer to Heather. I found a tiny screwdriver to dismantle an old case and a craft knife to slice the ends neatly and threw myself into it: winding the tape off the spindles, cleaning away mud and smoothing everything out. When my mum called me down for dinner, she asked what I'd been doing all afternoon.

"Messing about with tapes."

In many ways, it was all I'd been doing for years.

When I was ready, the tape went into my boombox with a blank alongside, copying, in case I managed to play anything. Finger hovering over pause, twitch-ready for the telltale garbled sound of the play head chewing up the tape, I pressed play.

It was that band, the rainy one. Our band. Our beginning. Not the first track on the album, but the third. I listened to it, tears rolling down my face, then laughed through them at the next track. Heather had flipped it the way I'd shown her, playing it backwards, then the fourth track, then the fourth track backwards. Comparing and contrasting her own flipped versions with the way the band had used backwards audio from one track to form the basis of the other. It was so exactly the sort of thing I would have done.

Heather's voice, squishy and thick, came out of the speaker: *thank you for the album*. She'd worked out how to say it so that it sounded right when played backwards—or right enough to be comprehensible. I knew how hard that was.

Was that what she'd wanted to play me? Had she recorded the message for me? Who'd thrown it under the wheels of the van?

I was slow, too slow, and by the time I hit pause, the next section of tape had crumpled up and snapped in the rollers.

I carried on winding the tape out, trying to smooth the hard folds away, wind it back in, repair the breaks. Dad chased me off to bed around one in the morning, and I spent all day Sunday on it, but I got almost nothing off the rest of the tape. The rest of side A was too damaged, and the one 'good' bit of side B was some Johnny Cash tracks we hadn't cared for.

All I had of Heather's last tape was the flipped songs and the message she'd tried to play me.

Just her voice, with the attack all wrong. Five words, each starting quiet and ending loud.

That was all I had of her.

I went to school. I sat through lessons. I sat under the stairs during breaks.

I kept expecting—hoping—Heather would suddenly be beside me, holding out her headphones to share something. Sometimes I'd see blonde curls vanishing around a corner and hurry after them, only to find some other girl, someone who looked nothing like her.

Thank you for the album.

Instead, I played her voice over and over and thought of her practising, recording her voice and flipping the tape—again and again until she got it right. For me.

Each day, I walked home past Heather's house. The van wasn't there, and every day I knocked on the door. No one answered. I looked around the sacks of rubble in the garden to see if there were any more tapes and peered through the letterbox, hoping I'd catch sight of something—anything—that would tell me where she was.

After about a week, Steve ducked under the stairs and sat down beside me. When he reached to push stop on my personal stereo, I let him.

"What's going on, Stu? What happened?"

"What do you mean?"

"Where's Heather?"

I shrugged. "Dunno. Isn't she here?"

He stared at me. "You know she isn't. She hasn't been here for nearly two weeks. Everyone's talking about it."

"Not to me."

He rolled his eyes. "Maybe because you spend all your time under here with your headphones on."

"So?"

He twitched away, like he was going to move, then sat back down.

"Look, Stu. A policeman came into Heather's class today. Asking if anyone knew anything. About where she'd run away to."

"Run away?"

"Apparently. I figured you'd know."

"Well. I don't."

"Aren't you worried about her?"

"Yes." Steve talking about it made it real, and I bit out as few words as possible. It didn't help. A tear was already sliding silently down one side of my nose.

He looked straight at me. "The policeman said Heather's parents reported a boy hanging about outside their house acting suspicious."

"I kept hoping she'd be there."

"You should probably tell the police."

"Yeah."

I agreed.

I should.

I didn't.

If the police didn't know where she was, I couldn't bear to talk to them. I had nothing to tell them.

I stopped going home via Heather's house.

The following day, Steve grabbed me after lunch. "Come on. Football."

I shook my head. It wasn't him; it was the curious eyes of the others. Had they all heard about the boy who hung around outside Heather's house? Had they guessed it was me?

"It's nice out." He pointed to the window.

"Nah. Not today."

He turned abruptly and headed for the playing field.

"Thanks, though," I called.

He paused, then carried on walking.

He didn't speak to me again for a couple of days. I existed in a daze, barely there, only coming to life when I made it back to my boombox. When I lay on my bed to listen, Heather's shadow lay down beside me, and I switched from one album to another to try to please her. All the music belonged to Heather.

On Saturday, I stayed in bed. Mum asked if I was ill, and I couldn't even face lying. No, I said. I just didn't want to get up.

I'd been awake till almost four, listening to the radio and hoping to find a new song, a special song, one that would bring Heather back. Mum left me for a bit, then came to tell me I was getting up and helping Dad mow the lawn. I hated the heavy push mower—why couldn't they buy an electric one?—so when Steve came by on his bike, asking if I wanted to ride up to the woods, I jumped at the chance.

Dad was surprised—Steve and I hadn't ridden around on bikes in a couple of years. He said my tyres would be perished, but they pumped up fine and we pelted along the track, away from town.

For a while I rode without thinking but, long before we reached the old bridge, I'd started trying to work out what to say to Steve. He'd been my friend for years, the person who knew me best. He'd badgered me with questions about Heather, then laughed and jeered at us, and I'd hated him for it. He'd told me about the policeman. And here he was now, reaching out, offering me something nostalgic. Something that didn't remind me of her.

He beat me up the hill, and by the time I dropped my

bike, he'd already scrambled past the bridge, into rough ground and broken concrete. The place wasn't pretty and didn't really have enough trees to be a wood, but we'd spent a lot of time here as kids. For a moment, I was almost happy.

Steve stood on one of the three upended sections of pipe, and I jumped on to another. It was a game we'd played a million times.

"One, two, three," Steve yelled.

We jumped, careering up the slope. As I slipped in the mud, Steve pulled ahead and suddenly we were both laughing—him up on the third pipe, triumphant, and me out of breath below. I kicked at a mass of old leaves and something bright snagged against my foot. Something yellow. A blonde curl.

"Steve!" I was on my knees, sweeping the leaves away. "Steve!"

By the time he'd jumped down, you could see her face. Her shoulders. Already I could tell from the lines of her collarbones that something was terribly wrong. Her plaid shirt was unbuttoned and her chest...

Her chest...

"Steve, there's..."

"What?"

"There's something wrong with her."

Steve's face was a hollow mask, his jaw working frantically.

"Something wrong?" he whispered. "Of course there is, she's dead. She's dead!"

"I know, but look." I scrabbled more leaves away, loose twigs snagging on her shirt and on mine. "Look!"

"She's *dead*!"

Steve's hands clawed my shoulders, dragging me back, his voice high and crazy in my ears.

"Stop touching her! She's dead, she's dead!"

Of course she was dead. Her hair was as sunshine-beautiful as ever, but her face was bruised grey and purple and crawling with pale maggots. Her skin had slipped and sunk in horrible distortions. Some part of me was not even surprised—but even decaying, she was still Heather.

My head pounded; my vision blurred. Steve's frantic screaming was muffled and distant. Slumped in the dead leaves, I stared at Heather. Not at her face, but at the point below her throat, where her chest had burst open to show the tight-packed mass inside her ribs. Spilling out onto the earth were hundreds upon hundreds of cassettes.

Steve left me beside her. He told them, later, that he tried to get me to leave. I guess he did. I remember his hands pulling at me, pulling at me, and the meaningless buzz of his voice. When he ran, the silence was a relief.

The scratched plastic tapes bulged out of Heather's chest, and I wondered about taking one, even stretched out my hand a few times. But if I'd picked up just one, I would have scooped them up by handfuls, cramming them into pockets and bundling them into my shirt, pulling what was left of her to pieces.

These were the last of Heather's tapes. There would never be any more.

Never again having the thrill of clicking play and waiting to see what she'd recorded would be devastating. I couldn't have taken just one, but I wish I had.

When the police arrived, I was still lying there, staring at Heather, indifferent to the things that crawled across me.

Someone led me away. I remember only a vague blundering from place to place and an endless parade of faces with troubled eyes. And questions. So many questions.

How had I found her, what did I know, why were we even in that area?

How did I know where she was, why had I brushed the leaves from her face, why had I stayed by the body?

And all I could say was, "Because she's Heather."

Did I go to the police station? I can't remember. Steve was there at some point, and he turned away from me, his face sick and terrified. Everything was irrelevant, because Heather was dead. Their voices were drowned by the hiss of static in my ears. Heather was dead, and all the music inside her was bursting out, and no one would ever hear it again.

There were always more questions, but never about the important things. Deep inside myself, I could hear the rainy whispering sound of the first song on the first mixtape and I sank into it, letting myself fall into the guitars and feeling the rhythm of the drums echo through my ears. I let it relax me into a place where I could pretend Heather was there beside me, ready to swoop and swap the tape the minute the song ended.

"Stuart!" My mother's voice was furious. "Stuart, you're not listening!"

Of course I was. Just not to them.

There were long days. Interviews and psychologists and endless retellings of details. My mother was a scratched record, imploring me to remember, to help, to *try*. Instead, I listened over and over to Heather's tapes in my head.

Without Heather, nothing mattered anymore. Not even me.

Eventually, someone declared it over. My mother wept, her arms roaming my shoulders. My father sniffed. "You're lucky," he said. "Lucky not to be charged."

Alone in my room and finally free, I stuck a tape into my personal stereo and turned the volume wheel as far as it would go. The whispering, raining notes poured over me.

"Our beginning," Heather had said. I wrenched the tape out, chose another, and another, pulling them from the shelves until my room looked like hers. Heather would have known the right song. Right for what? Our ending? Perhaps I didn't want to find it.

The next tape was labelled "Rolling Stones" in handwriting I didn't recognise, but instead something electronic and jarringly upbeat poured out. I flung it at the wall and picked up the tape I'd been making for Heather when she vanished.

Had I known? The first song stabbed into me, made my ribs ache with trying to hold everything in. Was that how Heather had felt when the weight inside burst out through her chest?

The second song was something I barely remembered. Why had I chosen it, what did I want to tell her? Could I divine my own mind by reading the message I sent her? When it ended, I put another in to play and searched my desk for the craft knife. I sliced the end of the last tape, reeling it out and sticking it back down so I could wind it all in backwards, find out if I'd left myself a message. Oh, Heather, would you have read my message? The tape shone in the dim light; the craft knife glittered. A chorus kicked me in the chest, leaving me gasping at how empty my world was.

When I drew the knife along the inside of my wrist, something dark and glossy gleamed back at me. I cut again, and it began to pour. It hissed gently in my ears as it flowed across the desk. Yards and yards of shiny magnetic tape heaping in coils as it drained from me, my life unspooling as I watched. I stared until it was too dark to see and even the guitars jangling in my ears faded away.

I wasn't there when they buried Heather. Nobody would tell me what music her family chose for her funeral.

"You need to focus on yourself," said Dr Gee, who came to see me a lot. He said many things, mostly about why they took my personal stereo away. As if that made any difference; the music was always in my head. It was inside me, just as it had been inside Heather. That's what scared me about the drugs they handed me: they might stop the music. At least Dr Gee would let me talk about Heather, but even he knew how he thought I should behave.

For a long time, I fought him, Heather's curls tossing through my mind. The way she jerked her head back to show contempt for authority. But he got me eventually:

I learned the best way to get his approval. I learned the things not to say. I even learned to enjoy silence.

When they let me out, school was over. Just like that. I'd missed it. My former friends were busy with their new college lives and looked at me sideways if we passed in the street. Not wearing headphones left me feeling naked and exposed, but I never heard the things I suspected they whispered.

Steve avoided me. He avoided me for years, even though we sometimes drank in the same pubs, and I was twenty before I spoke to him again. He was leaning against a wall, well after closing time, a pool of vomit by his feet.

I'd had a few myself, but he looked lost and alone.

"You all right, Steve?"

"Evening."

"Do you need a hand getting home?"

"Do you remember the day we found Heather?"

The question hit me like cold water.

"Do you?" His words were slurred. "Remember it?"

"Of course."

"I still dream about it."

I didn't. I still thought about Heather, but less often. Sometimes when I heard a song on the radio. When I saw a kid wrapped up in the music of their headphones. When it rained. But I never dreamed of her.

"I still wish I'd taken one of the tapes."

"Huh?" Steve's gaze grew more unfocused. "What tapes?"

"The tapes. In Heather's chest. They'd burst out. Her body was stuffed with tapes."

"What tapes?" he asked again.

"When we found her."

"You're a sick fuck," he said, then folded over, splattering his shoes and mine with more puke.

I spent days in the library, combing through the local newspaper archive, looking for the reports of Heather's death. I read a lot of untrue things about myself, about what I had said and how I'd acted.

Nobody mentioned the tapes.

Months later, I queued up at HMV to buy an album–their second album, Heather's rainy band. It'd been five years, and I barely listened to music anymore. By myself, there no longer seemed any point. But I bought this tape for Heather and walked up to the woods with my boombox. I played it for her and wondered whether it would feel like our ending. It meant nothing. I had no sense of whether

Heather would have liked it. The music was over—or perhaps it was me that was over.

When the button clicked up at the end, I let the silence take me. I embraced it, let my mind go blank, and allowed myself to drift away.

ABOUT THE AUTHOR

Elizabeth Guilt lives in London, UK, where history lurks alongside plate glass office buildings and stories spring out of the street names.

Her fiction has appeared in *Pseudopod*, *Escape Pod*, *Cosmic Horror Monthly* and various anthologies. She also presents the Drabbletober podcast, which releases daily micro-fiction during the month of October.

www.elizabethguilt.com

Thank you for supporting Graveside Press and our authors. One of the biggest ways you can help is to leave a star rating or a review wherever you purchased your copy!

Stay spooky.

Stay up to date with Graveside news and monthly free stories here!